*The
Rain-Cloud
Pony*

The Rain-Cloud Pony

by ANNE ELIOT CROMPTON
drawings by PAUL FRAME

Holiday House · New York

Library of Congress Cataloging in Publication Data

Crompton, Anne Eliot.
   The rain-cloud pony.

   SUMMARY: Pat seizes the chance to ride and care
for a horse even though she must deceive her parents
in the process.
   [1. Horses—Fiction]   I. Frame, Paul, 1913–
II. Title.
PZ7.C879Rai   [Fic]   76-47545
ISBN 0-8234-0295-9

1   The black stallion reared and snorted. His eyes flashed but I gentled him with a word.

I leaped on his back. My heels nudged his shining sides. He lunged forward, mane and tail streaming. He thundered down the street. Crouched low on his neck, I took the wind in my face.

Mom had called to me from the garden where she was spading. "Patty, ride down to the store? We're out of bread for lunch." So off we galloped, through the spring Saturday morning. Rusty was a gallant sight. He gleamed in the sunshine. His clattering hoofs sparked the tar.

But nobody gave him a second glance. Two girls I sort of knew from school waved to me.

A boy dashed across the street and never even looked at Rusty, who was charging toward him. And there was nothing strange in that. None of the people could see the black stallion at all. What they saw was a girl's rusty bike, with the fenders gone.

Last year, I started thinking horse. I day-dreamed about horses, running free in meadows. I saw them toss silky manes and prance. I watched them roll in warm, sunny grass. Where they rolled, the clover smelled sweet.

Back then, I did not want to have a horse. I wished I could be a horse. It would be great to have four strong, fast legs, a swishing tail, an arched neck! It would be great to feel beautiful! Naturally, I would be a wild horse. No one would halter me. Lying in the warm sunny grass of our old yard, I would look way up into the dizzy sky and dream about it. Then I would bring myself back to earth. "Pat," I would tell myself sadly, "there's nothing you can do to change it. You were just born human."

Then I decided that, if I couldn't be a horse, at least I could know all about them. I saved up my allowance and bought the Horse Book.

It's thick like a dictionary. It's got pictures on every page. It tells everything about horses— how to feed and breed and train them. Everything.

When I knew it all, I started hinting. I would say, "Rusty's got a flat tire. Now, a *horse* would never have a flat!" Or, "Look at all the cars stuck on the ice. Those people should sell their cars and buy horses!"

One spring morning, I sat on the outside stairs, thinking how much I wanted a horse. My dad came and sat with me. He lit his pipe, so I knew he had something to say. But it wasn't what I hoped.

"Pat," he said. "A horse eats a lot."

I said, "I'll get a paper route. He won't cost you a thing!"

"Pat." Dad puffed. "A horse needs a barn."

"I've got that figured out. He can live in the cellar. We just knock out the cellar stairs and build a ramp."

"Patty. We'll be moving again. Maybe next time we'll live in the city. A horse can't live in the city."

Dad couldn't see it my way.

I couldn't be a horse. I couldn't even hope to *have* a horse. I made do with Rusty. And nobody smiled or stared as I rode Rusty to the store, because they didn't know. All they saw was me, with hair in my eyes, and Mom's dimes jingling in my jeans, whooshing down the street.

A clicking noise followed me. It was Lad's toenails hitting tar.

Lad was brown and white, a kind of collie, twelve years old. I once figured that in dog time, Lad was eighty. He stayed home a lot, now, sleeping under my baby brother's carriage. But sometimes when I rode Rusty, he came along. He liked a run.

The street was a long strip on the edge of town. On my left, the town zipped by, gas stations and discount houses. On my right, the meadows rolled gently off to the country. The meadows were grassy hillocks, thickets, puddles and pools. A brook ran across the meadows. On a low hill beyond the brook stood our old house, where we lived last year. It gleamed white in all the green, like a dropped handkerchief.

8

Along the street, new houses poked up like mushrooms. Out at the end was the store, with a mud lot around it. I whizzed along with no hands, whistling, enjoying the sun. Even the mud lot looked clean in that Saturday sun.

Lad guarded Rusty while I went in the store. Coming out, I slung the bread in Rusty's basket and wheeled him to the tar. I was just about to mount, when I heard it. I knew what it was, right off. But I couldn't believe it.

I stood, with one hand on Rusty's handlebar and one hand on the saddle. I listened. "It can't be," I told myself. But it was.

Ta-lop, ta-lop, tla tla ta-lop. I stared up the street. I wasn't the only one.

The street was lined with kids. A boy yelled, "There she comes!" A little boy jumped up and down.

She came down the street like a silver rain cloud on dainty hoofs. She was little, maybe eleven hands. Her long mane lifted and drifted, cloud-white. Her little hoofs tapped the tar smartly, ta-lop, ta-lop.

She loomed nearer, and the thud of hoofs shook in my ears. I suddenly realized that this

9

was a good-sized animal, coming right at me. A wonderful smell of sweaty hide and leather came with her. I thought, "She's real!"

She ran up beside me. I looked into her wide, dark eye, not a yard from mine. Right then, I stopped being even a little scared. That eye was soft, like rich, brown velvet.

The pony was pulled up sharp. Tight reins jerked her head down. "Hey," I yelled at the rider. "You shouldn't stop fast like that!"

"Yeah?" The rider swung gracefully down, before the pony found her balance. "You know so much, you hold her. I'm going in the store."

The rider stalked off. I was left with the silver pony, in the midst of a gathering crowd.

Lucky I knew what to do. I stood Rusty on his kickstand. Then I grasped both reins in one fist, close under her chin, so that if she reared . . . She tossed her head and stepped away. I pulled down firmly on the reins, the way the Book said. The result amazed me. The pony stopped.

She was worth ten of me! I had felt her strength, pulling me along. But she stopped, shifted her weight, and blew startling, real spit all over me.

The leathery horse smell was like a mist around me. The pony's velvet eye stared softly into mine. The crowd of kids murmured and pointed. I felt their admiration and their envy. But I was too dazzled to be proud.

After a while, I dared to lift my free hand and touch the pony's smooth, damp neck. She did not seem to mind. I patted. Then I slipped my arm around her chin. We began to get used to each other.

Back came the rider, trailing smoke. She dropped a package of cigarettes into the pocket of her elegant red coat. "Thanks," she said shortly and took the reins. She mounted, fast and smooth. High in the squeaky new saddle, she looked very grand. She kicked booted feet into the gleaming stirrups. The pony half reared and stepped sideways. Her velvet eye lit up. I backed off and stumbled over Rusty.

I landed on my seat on the tar, all tangled up with pedals and handlebars. The crowd of kids laughed. Lad growled.

I looked up and saw the pony looming. The rider sat calmly, one hand on the pony's rump,

12

the other tight on the reins. She looked down at me from her noble height. "Sorry," she said. "Bonny's skittery."

I said right out, "She wouldn't be if you handled her right."

The girl smiled. She had a really strange smile. If you painted a smile on a Roman-goddess statue, it would look about that warm and friendly.

I sat in the middle of Rusty and licked my skinned palms and looked at her. I notice pretty people. I myself am far from pretty. My hair is brown and straight. I wear it short with bangs. My eyes are blue or gray, depending. My face is square, and I haven't any waist. So I notice pretty people. And I had never seen anything like this before. The girl wasn't pretty. She was beautiful.

She was tall and slim. She held herself proudly. She had golden curls which bounced on her shoulders and brown eyes that looked calmly out from under golden lashes. There was one fault with the whole glamorous image. Those calm, brown eyes were hard.

14

"Well, I'm sorry," she said again. "I'll get you another loaf of bread." I looked down, and there was Mom's loaf squashed flat under a hoof.

I looked again. "You don't shoe her!" I cried angrily. "You can't ride her barefoot on tar! How would you like——"

"O.K. O.K. Tell me tomorrow."

She sent one of the gaping kids into the store for bread. She got down and helped me pick myself up, also Rusty. "Shut your dog up," she said. "He makes me nervous." Lad was growling like a sick engine.

She tossed the new bread into my basket and never glanced at the kid again. I thought she could have offered him a ride!

"Come on," she said to me. "Let's get out of here."

She swung up into the creaking saddle and jerked the pony's head toward the street. The crowd opened before her. She kicked hard, and Bonny took off, showering stones and gravel behind.

I whooshed after them. In a minute, I was

15

gliding alongside the cantering pony. The white of her eye gleamed at me. I called up to the rider, "Is Bonny afraid of bikes?"

The girl smiled that cold-marble smile. "She's well trained."

We sped through the bright morning. Ta-lop, ta-lop went the pretty hoofs. Click, click went Lad's claws. Rusty's tires sighed on the tar.

The girl did not ask where I was going. She took it for granted that I wanted to go with her. We came to the driveway that led out across the meadows to our old house. The rider reined in suddenly. Poor Bonny stumbled.

"Here's where I live." I saw that the girl wanted me to be impressed.

I said, "I used to live here, last year."

"You did?" The big brown eyes widened a bit.

"Yes. When my dad was fixing it up to sell."

"Why'd he sell it?"

"That's what he does. He fixes old houses and sells them. We live in them, meanwhile."

She giggled. "You mean, that house was done over last year?"

"Sure was!"

"That's funny, 'cause we're still doing it over. Want to see?"

She kicked Bonny into a trot. I followed them up the long, long driveway. On either side, the meadows rolled green and wet. Wild ducks dabbled in the stream. We crossed the little wooden bridge, and the house loomed close, shining white. Set on a hill, with a pillared porch in front, it looked like an old Greek temple.

As Bonny jogged ahead of me, I noticed she was mighty fat. The Horse Book had a lot to say about fat. Must be the girl was feeding her wrong. I wondered if I should say so.

We rode up beside the house into a paddock, and Bonny stopped. She drooped, and her fat sides heaved. The rider leaped lightly down.

"This is new," I said, looking around. We never had anything like this! The paddock was a huge side of meadow, white-fenced. There was a little shed. The whole job was very neat, not home-done.

I was wondering if the girl would offer me a

ride. I had never been on a horse, but I thought I knew how. I had dreamed enough!

"Say," I began. Then I saw that she was loosening the girth. I stood Rusty up and went to help. We lifted off the saddle. It was tremendously heavy! Bonny sighed happily. Her sides flopped even fatter. Angel took the bridle off, and Bonny was left in her halter. She walked away, nosing grass. No ride this time.

"Come on in," said my friend-to-be. "I bet you'll be surprised."

"Stay," I told Lad. He didn't mind. He plunked down beside Rusty, panting and drooling.

We went in the back door and dumped the tack in the pantry. "My name's Pat Dunfield," I said.

One hand on the kitchen door, she glanced over her shoulder. "Angel Jason."

"*Angel?*"

"Angela. My dad calls me Angel. He says there's two kinds of angels. He can't decide which kind I am."

She showed me the kitchen. When we lived

here, this room was mostly storage. My dad piled panels here, with tiles, fixtures, French doors. Now the tile was on the floor, the fixtures were fixed, shiny-bright. It didn't look as if anybody cooked here. I looked about for Mrs. Jason. She wasn't around.

We saw the dining room. Dad's panels were covered with huge, dark paintings. "Portraits." Angel shrugged. "Ancestors." She had a lot of them. "Senator This. Governor That."

I looked about for Mrs. Jason. Nothing like wandering about in a stranger's house! But she wasn't around.

In the front, Dad had knocked out a wall and made two rooms into one. Angel said, "We might put a wall in here, have two rooms."

We went down to the Game Room. We had lived down there, while Dad fixed the house above us. We called it the cellar. Mom had made it homey, with chintz and linoleum. There was no chintz there now. Where my bed had stood, the Jasons had a bar. A TV took the place of Mom's stove. A pool table took up our "dining area."

Angel said, "Have a drag?" She pulled the pack out of her pocket.

I tried a drag. Angel watched me, waiting to laugh. But I didn't give her much to laugh at. I had practiced smoking before. Maybe I couldn't blow smoke rings like hers, but I could draw and puff and flick ash, like I knew what I was doing. I did get kind of dizzy and dry.

I said, "I've got to get home."

"In a hurry?"

"We're having that bread for lunch."

I left Angel sprawled on the couch, smoking. The game room was all blue haze from her smoking.

The outside cellar steps led up into Bonny's paddock.

She was out in the middle, moving slowly, nibbling. The noon sun shimmered on her gray, satin coat. The fat side toward me was dappled white, like water in sunshine. She swished her white tail, lifted her head and looked at me.

I called, "Good-bye, Bonny." I added, "I'll

be back and see you." I didn't think Angel would mind.

Bonny watched me. Her ears twitched. Her fat side heaved.

Halfway onto Rusty's saddle, I dropped back. Had I seen what I thought I had seen?

It happened again. Something inside Bonny shrugged and stretched. Something punched and kicked.

Should I rush back in and tell Angel?

Must be she didn't know, or she wouldn't ride around with that tight girth and heavy saddle!

But I wasn't sure. It would be embarrassing to be wrong. I'd better go home, look it up in the Book. If I was right, I'd hurry back and tell Angel.

I whistled to Lad. He grumbled, got up and stretched. I shut the paddock gate behind us, climbed onto Rusty and coasted off home. I rolled as slowly as I could, so old Lad wouldn't have a heart attack.

2   Our house didn't look like much. It was tall and thin and wedged in between two bigger houses. There was just room for Mom's garden, a tiny yard, and Dad's red pickup truck. As soon as Dad had the house painted and done up, we would sell it and move somewhere else.

But the homey feeling hit me as I turned into the yard.

I leaned Rusty against the wall. Lad flopped in his hole under the outside stairs. I grabbed the bread and ran upstairs to the kitchen.

In this house, we lived on the top floor while Dad fixed the first floor. There were inside stairs, but we mostly used the outside ones. Through the screen door at the top floated lunchy smells. As I opened the kitchen door, I heard bacon sizzling.

The kitchen was hot. The chairs and table were buried in piles of clean laundry, mostly diapers. My infant brother Marty gurgled and kicked in his crib. His gurgles were just beginning to sound hungry.

I leaned over the crib and pushed my finger into his fist. He stared up at me.

Mom was at the stove, lifting bacon strips out of popping fat. She wore gardening overalls. Her brown bangs flopped in her eyes, like mine. Her figure was squashy. She asked, "Bread?"

I tossed the bread on top of a pile of socks. Bread and socks tumbled on the floor, but I couldn't worry about that. Right then, Marty decided he was hungry. Looking up into my eyes, he opened his pink mouth and bawled.

"You get him, Patty." Mom went on spreading bacon on wrapping paper.

I eased my hands under Marty's back and sat him up. Right away he cut the uproar. Solemn as church, he wobbled and looked around. I kept a spread hand behind his back.

"How come you're so late?" Mom scooped up the bread, ripped it open and plunked four slices in the toaster.

"I met this Angel."

"Who?"

"Her name's Angel."

"A friend from school?"

"No. She goes to private. I stopped at her house."

"That's very nice." Mom was always wishing I would make more friends. She didn't know how hard it was, changing schools all the time. Everybody had their friends already. They didn't need me.

"Angel isn't really very nice." I decided this as I said it. "But Mom, she's got a——"

"If she isn't nice it doesn't matter what she's got." She shoved the laundry aside and set out plates.

"I know, Mom. But you don't understand. She's got a——"

"It isn't what you've *got*, Patty. It's what you *are*." Mom had to say it. She couldn't leave it alone. I was getting cross, fast.

I said loudly, "Mom! She's got a *pony*!"

Marty howled.

Mom lifted him up and away. His nose snubbed on her shoulder. His little fists jerked. "Talk softer around a baby, Pat. Pretend he's a horse. There's the toast. You butter it please?"

I had a story to tell, but Mom couldn't listen. I didn't exactly blame her, with Marty and the bacon and socks on the floor, and the kitchen shaking like an earthquake as Dad hammered downstairs. I didn't exactly blame Mom, but I did feel sort of left out and lonesome. I took my bacon sandwich to my own room, where I had friends.

My room was going to be the upstairs bathroom. It was almost big enough for my bed and table. On the table, the Horse Book lay open.

My friends ran and jumped and rolled on the walls. I cut out magazine horses and taped them up with my own drawings. I had snitched some famous horses out of old books, too. Traveller was there, with Bayard and Bu-

25

cephalus. Right over the table flew a red winged horse made of tin. He was just taking off, hind feet trailing. Wind whistled in his mane. He was free, without bridle, saddle or halter. In dreams, I used to ride him bareback through the clouds.

His label said MOBIL, but I knew better. His name was Pegasus. Pegasus was much grander than Angel's Bonny. He was noble. Bonny was

as ordinary as a living, breathing horse can be. Pegasus was wild and free. Bonny was very tame.

I shut my eyes and imagined flying on Pegasus. I pictured how the town would look from above. There would be roofs and antennas, chimneys and pollution. I saw clear sky, farther out. Pegasus and I would sail up into the blue. But now I knew what was wrong with

those sky rides. Pegasus did not sweat or smell of leather. His hoofs did not go ta-lop on the white cotton clouds.

I would have given all my Pegasus rides for one ride on real, fat Bonny!

I opened my eyes and bent over the Book. I must find out about Bonny. I looked in the index under "Breeding," . . . "Pregnancy," . . . "Foaling."

3   "Angel," I cried, "you can't use that saddle any more!"

Angel looked at me, down her Roman-statue nose.

"What are you talking about?"

It was Sunday. I had rushed over between Church and chicken dinner. The Jasons weren't having chicken. Through the open kitchen window, I smelled ham. They hadn't gone to church, either. Angel wore her red coat and boots. Bonny drooped her head by Angel's shoulder. They must have just come home from a long, fast ride. Bonny's coat shone wet.

"You can't use that saddle, it's too heavy. And the girth's too tight, it isn't good for her." As calmly as I could, I explained. I told Angel how Bonny's side had heaved and shrugged. I told her what the Book said about pregnant mares. "Mild exercise. No girth, no feed." Angel listened, blankly. She didn't seem surprised or even interested. Toward the end, I raised my voice. "Didn't you *notice* she was getting fat? *Look* at her!" I shook my finger at Bonny's round side.

Angel didn't bother to look. "O.K. But what's the good of a horse you can't ride? Good grief! I didn't want the thing, anyhow!"

"You didn't want . . ." What could she mean?

Angel held a stick in her hands. She started whacking it against her boots. Bonny jerked away. She would have run, if Angel hadn't held the reins.

Angel glanced at the open kitchen window. She lowered her voice. "See, they got me the horse so I wouldn't be thinking about other things. Get it?" She looked at me hard. "*Other things.*"

I didn't know what "other things" she meant. But I could see that Bonny would take up all a person's time.

"I didn't want it," she went on crossly. "It wasn't *my* idea. I have better things to do. I'm not horse-crazy, like you." Her face changed. Her eyes widened, then narrowed. She asked, "You don't want me to ride at all?"

"Not with a girth. Bareback might be all right." I felt proud, giving expert advice.

"Hmm." Angel tapped the stick slower against her boot. "I bet you're just jealous!"

"Oh no, it's true!" I had to make her understand. "It's all there in the Book. I saw the foal move, myself. Haven't you seen something move?"

"Sure." Angel smiled.

I stared at her. "Then why . . . why . . ."

"Like I said, I'm not horse-crazy. I don't care."

I exploded. "Angela Jason, you don't *deserve* Bonny!"

Bonny tossed her head, tugging at the reins. She didn't like anger or raised voices.

"Shhh." Angel nodded toward the window. "Listen, come over here a way, so we can talk. I've got an idea." She dropped the reins under

Bonny's nose and walked off.

"Wait a minute." I wasn't leaving Bonny cinched up like that! I walked bravely up to her. "Whoa, girl," I said. She stepped nervously away. Behind me, Angel laughed.

The Book said, "A horse will often stand still once it feels your hand." I went up to Bonny and laid my hand on her neck. The hot skin shivered under my touch, but Bonny stood still. "Whoa," I said again. I lifted my hand away. Bonny stood still.

I unbuckled the girth. Bonny heaved a deep sigh. Staggering, I lifted off the saddle. Then I drew the foam-slimed bit out of her mouth. I said, "Go on, now," and gently slapped her rump.

Bonny swished her tail and shook her loose halter. Then she walked away from me. I hugged myself. I had done all that by myself with a pony that didn't even know me!

Angel laughed. She had walked a good way out, away from the open window. As I came up to her she said, "O.K. Now, listen."

She told me that she had just come back from seeing her boyfriend.

"Boyfriend?" I asked. "How old are you?"

"Thirteen." Angel tossed her curls. "But he thinks I'm sixteen."

"Why, how old is he?"

She shrugged. "Eighteen."

"Eighteen?"

"Shhhh!" Angel glanced nervously back at the house. "He rides a Honda."

I searched my memory. Honda. Was it spotted? No, that was Appaloosa.

Angel flashed me a scornful look. "It's a *motorbike*, stupid!"

"Oh."

She whispered, "His name is Letty."

She went on to tell me how she used to ride Bonny downtown and tie her to a hydrant.

"In the hot sun?"

"Forget the dratted horse one minute and listen!" Angel and Letty would ride off on his Honda. Sometimes they rode for hours. Sometimes they stopped at a car-hop. (Bonny was still tied to the hydrant.)

34

This went on till one day Mr. Jason saw Bonny at the hydrant. Then there were questions, suspicions, a family quarrel.

I asked, "Why don't you just bring Letty home to see them? Say, 'This is my friend Let——'"

"Boy, you don't know much, do you!" Angel's brown eyes darkened with scorn. I looked away.

Bonny was rolling in the grass. Her hoofs pawed at the sky. She twisted and squirmed happily. Then she lurched to her feet, shook her mane and swished her tail. Her side heaved and pounded, as though she had twin foals inside.

"Pat, listen to me. Look at me. Pat, I've got it all figured out. It'll be great for both of us. I'll get to see Letty. And you, you'll get to ride Bonny!

"Now here's what you've got to do."

4   Pegasus snorted and stretched. His muscles rippled like surging water. Cold, fresh darkness flowed by.

I leaned over Pegasus' side and looked down into the night. Clouds drifted beneath us. Far below, town lights blinked like stars on a windy night.

I nestled down between Pegasus' wings. His mane lashed my face. My hair streamed, too, on the wind. Above me, the great wings beat.

Pegasus ducked and bowed into the wind. He turned a somersault and lay on his back on the wind. The town lights below wheeled above. Pegasus' hoofs waved at the sky. Clinging to his mane, I laughed out loud.

Laughing, I woke myself up. I was hunched

in bed between two wings of blankets. The window at my head showed pale gray. Next door in the kitchen, Marty whimpered. Mom talked gently. I heard Dad's heavy steps, and coffee pouring.

I lay still, coming down slowly. It must be almost six; they'd be calling me for school. As the dream faded, an uneasy feeling took its place. There was something coming up today, something not good. I didn't want it to be today.

Then it hit me. The pale light seemed to darken. If there hadn't been school, I would have shut my eyes and gone right back up on Pegasus.

I thought, "I'm not ready for today. I haven't decided." But today was here. Not to lie there and dread it, I got up.

"You're up early," Dad greeted me. "Busy day?"

"Mmmm." If only I could tell him about it. I sat down and poured my orange juice. Across the table, Marty's dreamy eyes watched me.

Cuddled to Mom's breast, Marty nursed

37

greedily. His waving hands brushed his hair and Mom's bathrobe. While he sucked and gulped, his eyes roved.

I don't know just what Marty saw. Dad said he saw lights and colors without understanding them. But Marty didn't mind not understanding. He was happy just seeing. Just being there in the day was enough for him. That morning, I envied Marty.

That morning, I even envied Lad! He sat by my chair. When I looked down at him, he flopped his tail against the floor. His soft bright eyes looked like Marty's. Neither of them had to decide about today.

The orange juice hurt my throat. Mom asked, "You feel O.K., Patty?"

"Oh sure." But the toast wouldn't go down.

Dad poured his second coffee and drank it fast. He sat up straight in his shirtsleeves, ready for action. He was sketching a design for a new bannister downstairs. "How's that?" he asked Mom. He tossed the pad over to her.

She looked at it over Marty's head. "Why

38

four inches?" she said at last. "Two and a half would do."

Dad scratched his gray-specked hair. He took the pad back and looked it over. "Right. Save thirty bucks." He ripped the sheet off the pad and started over.

I took the sheet and a pencil from his back pocket. While the toast cooled, I doodled. Maybe if I looked busy, they wouldn't notice my not eating.

I wanted so much to tell them, talk it over, get their ideas on it. But that wouldn't be fair to Angel. It was her secret.

Here was the thing. If I wanted to, *that much*, I could ride Bonny.

I saw myself galloping over the meadows. I would ride bareback, not to squash the foal inside. I would never kick or saw on the bit. Bonny would love me. (True, I had never been on a horse yet. That would be all right. Some things you don't have to learn. They are in you.)

If I wanted to *that much*, I could take care

39

of Bonny. I could brush her and feed her carrots. I could feel her soft nose on my palm. I could very nearly own Bonny.

But I would have to pay a heavy price, though not in money.

"How could they tell the difference?" Angel had whispered. "You'll look just like me!"

"My hair."

"Wear a scarf."

"My clothes."

"You can wear my red coat! They'll look out the window and see that red coat galloping around. And they'll say, 'How Angel does love that pony!'" She laughed. "And I and Letty will be miles away!"

I would have to help Angel fool her folks.

I argued it with myself, pro and con.

PRO: It wouldn't be my fault. I'd just go riding. Angel would tell the lies.

CON: I would be an accomplice.

PRO: How could it hurt? Bonny would be happy and taken care of. That would make it worth it.

"There." Dad tore off the second sheet. Getting up, he glanced at my doodles. "Nice. But horses' hind legs bend *back*ward. Like this." He showed me, drawing on top of my doodle. I had known there was something wrong with the hind legs. I did them over.

Dad went around the table and kissed Mom and the top of Marty's head. "When Hinton calls, tell him he can start bulldozing for the house foundation."

Mom said sadly, "I hate to see the meadows bulldozed!"

"I know what you mean. But somebody is going to do it. Those meadows are as good as gone. The town's going to swallow them, and we may as well profit. Have a good day, Pat."

Dad swung out of the kitchen and down the inside stairs. Pretty soon, we heard him ripping out the old bannister.

Mom asked again how I felt. I said, "Fine. Just not hungry."

I was hungry later. At school I bought two lunches! I sat by myself in a corner, watching everybody's backs, and worried.

PRO: Bonny needed love.

ANOTHER PRO: I loved Bonny.

CON: But I'd have to help Angel do something pretty bad.

ANOTHER CON: And there was no getting around that.

I sighed and gulped the second dessert. I didn't even know what it was!

Right after school, I wheeled Rusty out of the cellar. Mom was crawling about in her garden, poking out weeds. Marty kicked and gurgled in his carriage. Lad lay, panting, in the carriage shade. But when he saw Rusty, he thumped his tail and got up.

"Mom. I'm going over to Angel's."

"Whose?" Mom looked over her shoulder.

"The girl I met."

"Where's she live?"

"Our old house."

"Oh! You mean the *Jasons*!" Mom thought for a minute, holding her knife to the root of some poor weed. Then she said, "Well, all right. Be home by five." Jab.

I noticed how Mom said "Jasons." She wouldn't say Christenson or Lapointe or Pulaski quite that way. Wondering about it, I slid onto Rusty's saddle. We swished out onto the street. Lad came after us, panting and clicking.

At this time of day there was traffic. I was glad to turn off the street onto the Jasons' driveway. Farther on, I noticed a bulldozer charging around, growling. The bulldozer noises faded behind me as I coasted over the bridge. Wild ducks under the bridge made startled comments. Then I was pumping up the hill to the Greek temple.

When I used to come home here, there was sheeted furniture on the porch. Saws and hammers leaned against the pillars. The line dripped laundry. Now the line was gone. The porch was empty. The house seemed to frown at me.

I pumped up to the porch, drifted around the house and dismounted.

Out in the paddock, Bonny raised her fine Arabian head. I called to her. "Hey, Bonny!" She just looked at me and shook her mane. If I had her even a day, I'd teach her to come to me!

But I was here to see Angel, not Bonny.

I stood Rusty on the kickstand and let myself into the back pantry. Lad drooped along beside me. "Why did you come?" I asked him. "Why didn't you sit home? You're too old for all this running." He looked up at me and wagged.

I lifted my hand to knock on the kitchen door. Just then a man inside bellowed, "In public! On the steps of Town Hall!" My Dad had bellowed like that maybe three times in my life.

A tired-sounding woman said, "Doesn't matter. Who you think notish, anyhow?"

The man said roughly, "The whole town notices my family. You're public figures, like it or not!"

I almost knocked. Then I didn't knock. The man in there sounded pretty fierce.

The tired woman said, "Everybody does it."

The man growled, "Not my family!"

Glasses clinked. Then Angel said sweetly, "Never mind, Daddy. It was just tobacco."

I gathered my courage again and knocked.

44

Sudden silence. I heard the man's heavy footsteps cross the kitchen. Lad growled, even before the man jerked the door open.

Mr. Jason was big. He would have been good-looking if he hadn't been angry. Anger was a dark cloud around him. In one big hand he held a cocktail shaker. He glowered down at me. Lad barked.

Mr. Jason said, "Get that mutt out of here. Who are you?"

Behind him, Angel said, "That's my friend Pat."

"Pat," her father rumbled. "Get that mongrel outta here. Don't I know you?" He moved closer. I backed off, holding onto Lad's collar. Lad was going crazy.

Mr. Jason went on, "I've seen you with the dog. I've seen you on the street. You're Pat, eh?"

Angel edged past him, calmly blowing smoke rings. "Come on," she said to me, "Let's get out of here." Before her father slammed the door shut, I saw Mrs. Jason inside. She sat at the kitchen counter, drinking. Clouds of smoke eddied around her. She wore a shimmery dress. Her thin face looked old.

Angel led me outside. We leaned on the fence. Lad lay down beside me, still growling to himself.

"Well?" Angel widened her lovely brown eyes. She was almost as beautiful as Bonny! Our elbows touched. I knew if I said "yes," we would begin that moment to be friends. She would offer me a drag, and we would whisper together and laugh.

I said, "No."

"No?" Angel narrowed her eyes. A marble stiffness crept over her face.

"No, I can't do it."

I was trying not to look at Bonny. I couldn't bear to see her watching us. Now I would probably never see her again. But Angel looked over at her. She blew a perfect smoke ring.

"I thought you liked that pony there."

I confessed, "I love Bonny!"

"That's what I thought."

"But I can't fool your folks like that. Look, why don't you take Letty to see them——"

"You just heard!" Angel swung back to me. "You know what I did, got him so mad?"

Shoplifting? Pot? "What did you do?"

"Smoked on Town Hall steps."

"But . . . he *lets* you smoke!" I had just seen her smoking, right in front of her father.

"At home. Not on Town Hall steps. I have to look good in public. Pat, if he knew about Letty, he'd wring his neck! He'd knock his block off! He'd skin him alive!"

I shuddered. I believed her.

Angel squashed her cigarette on the fence and nodded at Bonny. "You're crazy about that pony, Pat. You'd better think this over again. I'm warning you."

5   What did Angel mean? I pedaled slowly home, wondering. The bulldozer stood in the meadow like a sleeping horse. The driver had gone home to supper. The traffic on the street had slowed to a trickle.

I wondered all through supper. Again, I didn't know what I ate! Mom asked me again how I felt.

I wondered through homework. I wasn't popular at school, but I was smart. I stayed in the top ten. That way, people at least knew my name. But that night I couldn't put my mind on sets.

What did Angel mean? "You'd better think about this again" was a clear threat. A threat of what?

Mom's voice floated in from the kitchen. She was singing to Marty.

> *Hushaby, don't you cry,*
> *Go to sleepy, little baby.*
> *When you wake, you will see*
> *All the pretty little horses.*

Very dimly, like a dream, I remembered her singing me that song.

I gave up on math. I sat there doodling between sets, thinking. How could Angel make me do what she wanted?

If we were bad guys in a Western, "You'd better think about this again" would mean trouble. Not trouble for me, trouble for Bonny. "You're crazy about that pony."

> *Blacks and bays, dapples and grays,*
> *Coach-a-four of little horses.*
> *Hushaby, don't you cry,*
> *Go to sleepy, little baby.*

What could Angel do to Bonny? Bonny was her jewel! And in a little while she would have

50

two of them, two live jewels. She would be the
envy of the town!

> *When you wake, you will see*
> *All the pretty little horses.*
> *Blacks and bays . . .*

Mom sang softer. Pauses came between
lines. I knew Marty was falling asleep. With
one hand he was patting his cheek, while his
eyes slid shut.

> *Hushaby, don't you cry,*
> *Go . . . to . . . sleepy . . .*

I was almost asleep myself. My head had
sunk to the table. I was nodding into a dream
about little horses. And there were horses
drawn all over the math.

No, Angel couldn't do a thing to Bonny. And
she couldn't do a thing to me, except not be
friends. I wasn't that sure I wanted to be
friends, anyhow.

Dad came in to say goodnight. The homey
smell of pipe tobacco came with him. He sat
on my table and nodded at the math. "Horses

are pretty good," he said. " 'Course, they aren't perfect."

"Why not?" They looked perfect to me.

"Can I draw on this? Look." Dad doodled a quick little horse. Under its stomach and under its feet, he scribbled dark. Instantly, the horse rounded out. It wasn't flat on paper anymore. It was round, as if it breathed air. Dad scribbled dark under its mane, and the mane flopped out thick. He said, "Shadow makes sunlight." The little horse shadowed the grass. Sunlight poured down on its back. I looked at it, longingly.

"Better copy your sets over," Dad said. "They all come out the same, did you notice?"

He was right. They were all different ways of coming at the same answer.

6   "Patty, run! Come quick!"

Tuesday after school, I was chewing my pencil over a composition called "Hobbies." Mom's shouts reached me from the garden.

For Mom to yell, it had to be important. I leaped up, brushing "Hobbies" all over the floor, and rushed out.

From the top of the outside stairs, I saw Mom kneeling in the garden. She was craning her neck to look down the street. Lad, by Marty's carriage, was thumping his tail. His ears cocked and wavered.

"What, Mom?" I yelled.

"Horse coming! Hear it?"

Now I heard it. Ta-lop, ta-lop echoed down the street. The horse was still out of sight behind the house. If I ran downstairs, I would see it close up. Where I was, I would have a better overall view. Ta-lop, ta-lop. Louder, closer. I ran down.

First came an escort of kids on bikes. I knew most of them from school. They drifted happily by, no hands, figure eights. Then came a running escort of little kids. All of their faces were bright with hope. Surely the horse would give them a ride!

Those ta-lops were close, now, but too soft. I knew before I saw. That horse wasn't shod.

Bonny cantered heavily past the house. Her head swung low. The girth was yanked so tight, her sides ballooned around it. Her satin hide was drenched in sweat.

Red-coated Angel rode elegantly. Her bright curls flopped in the sunshine. One hand rested lightly on Bonny's rump. But no happy excitement showed in her face. It showed only dreamy pride.

I shouted, "Angel! You can't do this!"

I lunged for the bridle. Bonny's sad eye watched me hopefully. At the last second her head was jerked away. She bumped against me, knocking me back. She galloped on, slowly, but too fast for me.

I was too mad to shout again. I was almost too mad to breathe. Watching poor Bonny jolt away, I felt every ta-lop as though I was the foal inside!

Angel never looked back. Rounding the curve, she started to kick impatiently.

That was too much.

"What a pretty sight!" Mom commented. "Where are you going?"

"Gotta catch her!" I ran to the cellar and wheeled Rusty out.

"But your hobby compo——"

"Please, Mom! I gotta!" I rushed Rusty onto the street so fast, old Lad never even noticed.

I zoomed around the curve. Ahead, the escort parties were breaking up. Little kids turned back, hot and disappointed. Bikes zigzagged and turned. Bonny was cantering off across the meadows.

At least she was off the tar. That squishy meadow grass must feel good. I couldn't catch her, that was sure. I wobbled around and pumped hard.

I zoomed back past our house. I just glimpsed Mom's back in the garden, and Lad scratching himself. They didn't see me. I pumped hard along the street to the Jason turnoff. I zipped over the bridge in a flurry of startled ducks. Momentum carried me coasting right up to the Greek temple.

Away out in the meadows, a silvery horse rocked toward me. I dropped Rusty clattering in the driveway and ran.

Pools and hillocks slowed me down. I turned my ankle and fell and scrambled up again. As I jogged nearer, Bonny slowed. Angel stopped kicking. She rode easily, loose as her bouncing curls. Panting, I stumbled closer. Now I could see Angel's marble smile.

Bonny and I trotted together. I fell against her. She dropped her nose on my shoulder. Both of us heaved and gasped. Angel sat, smiling.

When I caught my breath, I squeaked, "How could you!"

"I told you you'd better think it over."

I unbuckled the girth. Bonny heaved a deep, deep sigh.

Smiling, Angel asked, "Well?"

"Oh, I'll do it! I'll do it!"

"I thought you would."

"So now I'm in charge of Bonny."

Angel nodded.

"Get off! Hear me, get *off*!" I grabbed her sleeve and yanked her down. The loose saddle tumbled down with her.

She glared at me. "You're in charge. You bring the saddle." She stalked off home.

I called after her, "Your dad's right! There *are* two kinds of Angels!" She didn't seem to hear.

Tenderly, I drew the bit out of Bonny's mouth. I piled the tack on her back and tied the whole mess on lightly. Then I took her halter under the chin, the way the Book said. Gently, I urged her forward.

We traveled slowly. The tack slid about on Bonny. Once it fell off. We had to keep stopping. Bonny was much too tired to object to anything. She led along as gently as a pretend horse would. This was great luck for me. I had never led a horse before.

I guided her carefully around rocks and mud puddles. Her little hoofs thudded ta-thunk, ta-thunk in the grass. Her head bobbed quietly at my shoulder. The thought came to me, "I am leading a pony." I went hot with joy.

I was leading a live pony over real grass. Soon I would rub her down, feed and water her. And tomorrow, I would ride!

That night I heard Mom say, "Patty seems happy. She's been smiling to herself all evening."

I wrote a fair composition, called "Hobbies: Horses Are the Best." When I slept, I dreamed of riding. I rode Bonny, not Pegasus. We traveled the meadows, not the sky.

7 Some things you don't have to learn. They are in you.

It was just like my dreams. There were a few little details I hadn't thought of. Bonny's mane, flopping at my knees, was coarse and thick. Its smell mingled with the rich smell of hide and crushed grass. The reins were hard leather; they hurt my hands. I grabbed them fearfully, as though they could keep me from falling. Then I learned to grab the mane when I started to slide. For I rode bareback. No shiny leather creaked under me. No stirrups steadied me.

At first, Bonny stood quietly, waiting for a signal from me. I was too dazed and happy to move. I just sat like a queen on a throne.

Then Bonny decided if I had no plans, she did! My seat lurched. One side sank, the other side rose. I tightened my grip on the reins and clamped my feet hard against slippery hide. The coarse, white mane lowered itself toward the ground. I looked down Bonny's neck into grass.

Bonny nibbled. She munched, stepping forward slowly. My feet scrambled against her sides. The ground was way down there. Her feet touched it. Mine dangled.

Then I remembered the reins. Gently, I pulled them up and back. Bonny's head came up. Grass hanging from her mouth, she looked back at me.

"It's me," I said, shyly.

She chewed, watching me. Finally, she turned around front and stood, waiting.

I remembered what the Book said. I pressed with my heels. At the same time, I lifted the reins in one hand. "Tluck-tluck," I said, feeling foolish. The result was amazing! Bonny lurched forward. Her mane bobbed, her ears twitched. Between those ears, I saw the meadows roll slowly toward and under us. We were walking straight ahead.

It was like my dreams. I knew what to do. I rolled with Bonny's lurches. Swaying as she swayed, I balanced more easily at every step. My feet relaxed. I loosened the reins. "She neck-reins," Angel had said, last thing. I was proud I knew what she meant and didn't have to ask.

Rocks jerked by. Mud pools, mossy hillocks and hollows slid past. A very slight wind fanned my face. Warming up, I said, "Hey, Bonny! Let's go faster." Her ears twitched, but she just kept walking.

"Oh." I pressed with my heels and lifted the reins. "Tluck-tluck."

Bonny's tail swept grandly from side to side. Her head came up high. I was tossed from shoulder to shoulder, from neck to croup. "Hey! I didn't mean to trot!"

Then I remembered the Book. Clapping my knees tight, I lifted my seat in the air. That was a lot better. Now I had to bob up and down at Bonny's speed. I managed that. And it was as

63

if I had been doing it forever. Nothing to it!

Nothing but joy.

Now the wind whistled by us. It tugged at my scarf. I reached to tear off the silly scarf. Just in time, I remembered and left the scarf tied. The Jasons might be watching from a window. "Isn't it nice, how Angel likes to ride!" The scarf and the hot, red coat were my riding-rental fee.

A strip of greener grass bobbed near. We came to the stream. A flock of brown and green ducks paddled about under the bridge. If I had come on foot, like a human being, they would have squawked and leaped into the air. But we came on four legs, pressing earth gently, breathing grassy breath. The ducks dabbled and dunked, minding their own business.

Bonny waded in, bent her head and drank. For a minute I sat happily, watching the water swirl brightly about her fetlocks. But the Book said a sweated horse should not drink. Bonny was far from sweated, but I was taking no chances! I pulled her head up and turned her toward the bank. "Tluck-tluck."

We thunked slowly along the bank. I watched the ducks. They swam, waddled, preened on the bank. They paid no attention to us. The air flowed about us and the sky and earth ringed us.

We came to the bulldozer's new road. It was spoiling the brook. Dad had stuck a little pipe under the road, but it didn't help much. Bulldozed earth and stones were filling in the stream. I wondered what the ducks thought about it.

We walked a way up the new road. I liked the hollow thunk of Bonny's hoofs on hard dirt. But I saw she didn't like it. There were lots of little stones and gravel to catch in her hoofs. So I guided her back to the grass.

I nudged her sides. "Tluck-tluck-tluck." Her tail swished mightily. Her ears turned forward. She trotted a few steps, then broke into a canter.

We flew. I leaned low on Bonny's neck. I had no fear of falling. Bonny and I together were one being. Dirt and grass, stones and

mud bounded below us. We saw a stone coming and tensed for a leap. We sailed over and landed and went on, ta-thunk, ta-thunk. Wind whistled by us. Away ahead, the Greek temple bounced on its hill. It seemed too small to notice in the sweep of meadow and sky.

It was lovely to have four strong, swift legs, a swishing tail, an arched neck! It was great to feel beautiful!

The wind whistling in my scarf must have drowned out the noise of the car. I heard nothing but Bonny's ta-thunks, until the car honked.

We were cantering close by the Jasons' driveway. A big, shiny car had stopped halfway up. I knew the driver. He was big and would have been good-looking, except for the cloud of anger he carried. He waved impatiently at me.

I thought, "It works!" The red coat and scarf made a real disguise. "He thinks I'm Angel!" We cantered along, watching the car from the corners of our eyes. Mr. Jason honked again. "He wants me to stop!" I realized it with horror. "He wants to talk to me!"

There was only one thing to do. I pretended I hadn't heard or seen him. I lifted the reins high and left of Bonny's neck. She swung right. I leaned forward and nudged, and she speeded up even faster. We rushed across the meadows, away from the car.

8   "Well, of all the dummies!" Angela scolded. "I thought you'd know enough not to ride close to the house like that!"

"Aw, come on. How's Pat to know when your old man comes home?" Letty stood up for me. I think. It was hard to be sure. You couldn't see his thoughts in his face. All you saw was easy good temper. He smiled to himself a lot.

Angel said, "Well, next time ride out in the field. Anywhere but right beside the driveway!" She climbed off the Honda, a bit stiffly. "Here's your coat. Gimme mine."

Letty watched us exchange coats and scarfs. Smiling, he asked Angel, "When's next time, doll?"

Angel tossed her curls a bit before tying on her scarf. "When can you come, Pat?"

"Me? Oh. Tomorrow!"

Letty nodded. He gave me a smiling salute. Then he kicked on his motor and pushed off. As the Honda roared away, Bonny trembled. I patted her neck, and she blew warm breath on my hands.

"She's really well trained," I told Angel. "That Honda must have scared her, but she stood still."

Angel shrugged. "I didn't train her." (I was sure of that!) To my surprise, Angel added, "You want to come back with me and rub her down?"

"Your folks would see me!"

"So what? So long as they don't see you in my coat."

The three of us walked up the long driveway together. I led Bonny over the bridge. Then Angel took the reins. "Might look funny, you leading." I kept a friendly hand on Bonny's rump.

Angel was nice. She talked to me over her

shoulder in quite a friendly way. "This is a great system, don't you think so, Pat? How'd you like it? Did you get thrown?"

"Oh, no!" I was still ride-happy. I still felt earth and sky ringing me, wind rushing by. I liked Angel. I said chattily, "Letty's good-looking."

"He's all right," Angel swaggered. "If he wasn't, I wouldn't go out with him."

"Is he nice?"

"Depends what you mean."

"I mean, what does he talk about?"

"Talk!" Angel snorted. "Letty isn't the talking type, Pat. Letty's the doing type."

"Oh."

Back in the paddock, I rubbed Bonny down. I hauled her water and fetched a carrot out of my coat pocket. I held the carrot on my flat, open palm, the way the Book said to. Bonny's soft lip pushed against my palm and wiggled over it. She nipped up the carrot. Her powerful jaws crunched it to juice. "There, Bonny," I said, "Isn't that good!" I enjoyed it with her.

Angel laughed.

I didn't ride every day. Angel didn't want to see Letty that often. "I might get tired of him," she said. But I made her promise not to ride Bonny herself and not to give her feed. "She's too near foaling."

"O.K. with me." Angel shrugged.

The days I rode in Angel's hot, red coat, I rode more slowly. The foal moved a lot. Sometimes it would push against my leg as I rode. And Bonny seemed happy to plod around the meadows. The Book said: "The mare in foal needs mild exercise." I gave Bonny milder and milder exercise. I wanted to canter freely through the bright spring air. But I had to take care of that foal!

I wondered why the Book said "mare in foal," when actually the foal was in the mare. But I liked the sound of it. I told Dad, "The Jasons' pony mare is in foal."

"Ah. I see." Dad leaned against my table and brought out his pipe. That meant he felt like talking. I laid my pencil down.

"I see," said Dad again. "I've been finding

72

drawings crumpled up. Like this one." He showed me a scrunched-up sketch. "I wondered what they were all about."

I had been copying diagrams from the Book. They showed the foal inside. This one showed the right position, nose on front hoofs, ready to go. Another diagram showed the breech position, tail first. That might be bad. Another one showed the foal jammed sideways. That would be awful. I was getting worried. If anything went wrong, what would I do?

"You'd call the vet," Dad told me. "Or rather, the Jasons would. It's their pony. Why are you worrying?"

I told Dad some of it. I said Angel didn't care for her own pony. "And Mrs. Jason drinks all the time, she's no help."

Dad raised his speckled eyebrows. "All the time?"

"She has a cocktail for breakfast."

"I see." Dad puffed blue smoke.

"And Mr. Jason isn't there, most times. He wouldn't help anyhow. It's pretty much up to

73

me." My voice trailed off. Dad was looking at me hard, through the smoke. His eyes were full of questions.

Quickly, I changed the subject. "There's something important the Book doesn't say."

"What's that?"

"Look here." I flicked to the diagrams. "See, here's how the foal starts out. He's smaller than an apple seed."

"Yes."

"And here's how he grows. Ears, eyes, brain, hoofs. Did you know his hoofs are soft?"

"No, I didn't know that."

"They're soft like sponges, till he's born. They turn hard in the air."

"Ah."

"But what it doesn't say is, 'How does it know?' "

Dad puffed and watched me. I tried again. "How does this seed-thing know how to be a horse?"

Dad puffed. After a while he asked, "Did you see the lettuce in Mom's garden?"

Mom had made sure we both saw it. She

was awfully proud of those teensy green leaves. She was as excited about them as she was about the tulips sprouting under the stairs.

Dad said, "How does a lettuce seed know how to be lettuce?"

"That isn't the same at all!"

"It isn't? Why not?"

"Because . . . because . . . a horse . . ." A horse is bigger than lettuce. A horse runs around and neighs and rolls. Lettuce doesn't grow a brain!

Dad said, "I thought you got A in Life Science."

"Oh, that's no help! There's a chemical code in the genes. Fine. But, who writes the chemical code? And who reads it?"

Dad puffed. "I thought you got a gold star in Sunday school."

Impatiently, I picked up my pencil. "Where can I look it up?"

"Nowhere."

"You mean nobody knows?"

"Nobody who writes books. Fact is, Pat, lettuce and the foal and you, you're all mysterious fantasies." He pushed himself off my table and turned to go. "And don't you worry yourself about the Jasons' pony. Let them worry!"

I called after him, "I wonder how big the foal will be? Bigger than Lad?"

He laughed, trailing smoke. "Not much bigger!"

Lad was unhappy. He looked sadder every time I wheeled Rusty out of the cellar. I couldn't take him to the Jasons'. Mr. Jason knew him. He called me "the dog girl." I would say, "I'm sorry, Lad, but you've got to stay home." Lad would lie down by Marty's carriage and lay his head on his paws. He would look like crying.

"Poor Lad!" Mom said. "I don't think much of this Jason business, myself. Do they really let you ride their pony?"

"Not just ride. I get to feed her and brush her and——"

"Do they pay you for all this work?"

"Pay!" I stopped short, in the middle of folding a diaper. Mom ironed and I folded. Marty fussed in his crib. It was the first really hot day.

"Goodness, Mom! I should pay them!"

"For letting you work?"

"It's fun. It's almost like having my own pony."

"Well. I know how you've been wanting one. Now I guess you have it."

I finished folding the diaper and looked at her. She looked as hot as I felt. Sweat gleamed on her face. She swung the iron over a crinkled diaper. It came out all smooth and hot, and she tossed it to me.

"What do you mean?" I asked. "Now I have it?"

"Why, you love that pony!"

"Ugulu," Marty called.

"Loving isn't having," I said.

"It isn't what you have, Pat, it's——"

"Oh, I know, I know!"

"Not quite." Mom pursed her lips at my crossness. "I wasn't going to say what you thought, that time."

"Awaaaa," Marty shouted. The bassinet shook, as he wiggled and waved.

"I'm sorry. What were you going to say?"

"I was going to say, before you interrupted . . ."

"Waaaaa," Marty yelled.

"It isn't what you have, it's what you love. You take over, Pat. Marty can't wait any more for lunch." Mom went over to Marty. "Oogoo woogoo, is it hot? Is it wet? Throw us a didie, Pat."

I flung a hot diaper across the table. What was the good of washing and ironing the things? The minute we had a clean, smooth diaper, Marty went and wet.

I picked up the iron. Ripping noises came from downstairs. Behind me, Mom was changing Marty. "Oowee, lovely, doesn't that feel better?" She mumbled through pins. "Marty's mine because I love him."

I said, "Love's got nothing to do with owning."

"Loveum!"

The iron was heavy. My back ached. The pile of diapers went on and on. "When you're through," Mom said behind me, "would you ride to the store? We're out of mayonnaise."

At last, I smoothed the last diaper and unplugged the iron. Mom sat behind a swaying high-rise of diapers, nursing Marty. He waved his hand, stroking air. His glossy eyes watched me dreamily.

"Take the dollar out of the teapot," Mom said, "and take Lad along with you. I hate to see his face when you leave him alone. How come the Jasons hate dogs?"

So Lad came too. It was good to hear his claws clicking on the tar behind me. It was like old times. But he was out of practice. Pretty soon he was panting and dangling his tongue. I braked and wobbled along slow.

A lazy, warm breeze fanned my face. It was noon. There was almost no traffic on the street. I drifted past the Jasons' turnoff. Farther on, I stopped to watch the bulldozer. It was through road building. Now it was digging a new cellar hole for a house. A low hill hid the cellar hole from the Greek temple. I wondered how the Jasons would like having neighbors so nearby.

A car coming toward me slowed down. It

stopped alongside. The driver yelled, "Hey, kid!"

He wriggled over to the passenger side and poked his red face out the window. He was Mr. Jason.

"Hey, kid, I know you! What's the name again?"

I swallowed and croaked, "Pat."

"Eh? What's your name?"

"Dunfield."

"Pat Dunfield, that's it. I know your dog." He jerked his head at Lad. He seemed nicer this morning. Maybe he didn't drink in the morning.

"Listen," he said, "I'm looking for my Angel. You seen her?"

I shook my head.

"Lately, she's gone pony-mad. Rides all the time. We thought maybe she was out riding. But the pony's there in the paddock."

I shook my head.

"Well, if you see her, tell her we want her home. Hey, Pat. Didn't I see you the other day on a cycle?"

I started to shake my head.

"With a fellow. Sure, you had on that plaid scarf."

I mumbled.

Mr. Jason said kindly, "Kid, you want to watch out. I wouldn't trust my Angel with that oaf, I'm telling you now. If I caught him with my Angel, I'd wring his tough neck for him!"

I gurgled.

"You want to be careful, Pat. Oh, and another thing. It isn't that I don't like dogs or anything. But you know what a dog can do to a new lawn? You keep that mutt there off my place. You come see Angel, mess with the pony. But leave your mongrel home."

He waved, started up and drove past. I pushed off. I was alone again with the hot light, the breeze and Lad's clicking steps. "Where was Angel?" I wondered. Had she gone so Letty-crazy she couldn't wait for me to cover for her?

I bowled gently along to the store, wondering.

9   "I wouldn't trust my Angel with that oaf, I'm telling you now!" I wondered about Letty. What was he like, behind that loose smile? I thought of his eyes. They were cool gray. They took the world in and gave nothing back. I thought of his hands. They were always jammed into huge gloves. Letty went armed, like a knight. Letty on his Honda was very like a knight on a charger. Was he the hero knight, who rescues the maiden? Maybe he was the villain who carries her off.

Suppose something really bad, hard-to-imagine bad, happened to Angel. Would it be my fault?

"What do you think?" I asked Bonny. She

twitched her ears to show she heard me. She liked me to talk.

I talked to Bonny a lot. I would walk around the meadows, like now, talking. And Bonny would follow my voice. Her little hoofs ta-thunking, her tail swishing, she heeled as well as Lad. I didn't need to lead her at all.

This time, we were walking around the new cellar hole. It was deep, muddy, big. Dad and Mr. Hinton could build a castle on it. From where we stood, on the edge of the hole, we couldn't see the Greek temple at all. It was behind the near hill. So Mrs. Jason couldn't look out and see us, either. I slipped off the hot, red coat. The air felt good on my arms.

"What do you think?" I asked Bonny. "Would it be my fault if something happened to Angel?"

Bonny tossed her head.

"You don't care? Can't say I blame you."

I started off toward the street. It was time to meet Angel. "Hey, Bonny!" I swung around. Bonny wasn't following. She looked absently off into space. Her sides heaved a heavy jig.

"You don't want to walk, huh? You want to go home?" I went back to her. I took her Arabian head in my hands and looked into her eyes. "Bonny, do you know what that is, kicking inside?" Bonny stared peacefully back at me. She didn't know.

I patted her sleek neck. "Come on, we'll go meet Angel. Then you can go home." I turned my back and walked firmly away. Pretty soon, I heard ta-thunk, ta-thunk at my heels.

We waded across the brook. Ducks dabbling among the cattails went on dabbling. They knew us, by now. The splashing water sprayed us, making us cool. Swinging my sneakers by the laces, I came down to the street.

The Honda leaned on its kickstand in the roadside weeds. Something moved in high grass. A blond head popped up. "Here she is," said Angel. She knelt up, combing her hair.

Letty lay on his back, puffing smoke rings. "Always on time, Pat, huh."

"Angel," I said right off, "Bonny's going to foal any day."

"Your Book say?"

As a matter of fact, it did. Bonny showed all the signs the Book listed. But I said mysteriously, "Never mind, I know. I want you to call me when it happens."

"What are you going to do about it?"

I shuddered. "All right, call the vet. But you've got to have an eye on her, Angel."

Angel shrugged. "If I'm here."

"Why, you aren't going anywhere, are you?"

"Letty and me, we might go somewhere."

Letty giggled.

"You aren't running away!" I wondered if that would be a hard-to-imagine bad thing and my fault.

"Hm. That's an idea." Angel turned to Letty. "Shall I run away?"

Letty scrunched out his reefer. "Not permanent, doll. Can't afford that."

She turned sulkily back to me. "O.K., Pat, I'll watch your four-legged friend for you. I'll call you. *You* call the vet."

"Mom," I asked as we finished the supper dishes, "how do I find a vet in the phone book?"

"Vet of Foreign Wars? The Legion?" Mom wrinkled her forehead under her limp brown bangs.

"A veterinarian for Bonny."

"Oh, ah! Yellow pages."

Dad looked up from Marty. He sat by the table, jiggling Marty on his knees. "I told you, Pat, that's the Jasons' problem. Why are *you* involved?"

"The Jasons won't do it," I told him. "Angel asked me to call the vet."

"Oh? And who pays the bill?"

I hadn't thought of that.

"Just so it isn't me," Dad warned. "It's all I can do to finish this house and contract the new one."

He and Mom talked on about money. I heard "cellar hole," "foundation," "backhoe," "meadows." I was too hot to listen. I looked under V in the yellow pages. I wrote down a number on scrap paper and stowed it in my jeans.

The night was dripping hot. Marty fussed and squirmed. "He needs a nice cool bath,"

Mom said. She filled the Bathinette on the table.

Dad said, "If it rains, Hinton can't dig tomorrow. Whole area needs drainage."

"Forecast says rain." Mom lifted Marty off Dad's knees.

Lad and I went outside and sat on the top step. Down there in the misty, heavy dark, Mom's lettuces were greening up. They were almost big enough to thin. Under the stairs, the tulips had buds. You could see what colors they would be. I thought of all the plants sucking in damp heat, unfurling, stretching. Cars flashed by on the street. Kids rode by on bikes, shouting. Only I was alone in the hot dark.

I got up and went back inside, where there were lights and voices.

Mom lifted dripping Marty out of the Bathinette. "Pat, you hold him." I should have known. The minute Mom saw me, she had a job ready for me. "I'll see if his clothes are dry." She ran out and down the stairs to the clothesline. I sat at the table, holding Marty packaged in the bath towel.

He wiggled and looked about. I guess my arms didn't feel safe, like Mom's. My lap wasn't squishy. Marty screwed up his soft face and opened his mouth.

Hastily, I sang:

Hushaby, don't you cry,
Go to sleepy, little baby.
When you wake, you will have
All the pretty little horses.

Marty watched my mouth move. His face smoothed out.

Blacks and bays, dapples and grays,
Coach-a-four of little horses.

Mom thudded up the stairs. Her arms were full of clean laundry. "Be there in a minute." She vanished into the bedroom.

Hushaby, don't you cry,
Go to sleepy little baby.
When you wake, you will have
All the pretty little horses.

90

"No he won't." Dad took the pipe out of his mouth. "He can *see* all the pretty horses in the world. But he sure as heck won't *have* them, unless I sell these two houses and a couple more." He winked at me and stuck the pipe back in.

Mom came back, pinning the damp bangs off her forehead.

"It's 'you will *see*,' Pat. That's how I always heard it." She lifted Marty off me.

> *When you wake, you will* see
> *All the pretty little horses.*

"There now, isn't that nicer?"

In the night, I woke up sudden. Something roared by the house. "Tornado!" I thought. I went all stiff with scare. But the roar passed and faded down the street. "Motorcycle." I relaxed.

Then I heard thunder. Away over the meadows, thunder growled and snarled, pacing the sky. "Rain coming. Cooler." Happily, I pulled the sheet up over me and went back to sleep.

I dreamed a drawing. A pencil drew Bonny with the foal inside. It drew the nose lying on the soft front hoofs, and the long back legs trailing. The foal was all set to be born.

Then Pegasus snorted and stretched. His muscles rippled. I leaned over his side and looked down into the night. High as a hawk, Pegasus soared over the meadows. He circled like a hawk, slowly, tipping with the wind.

Down in the rainy dark, the meadows glowed weird green. A little gray rain cloud bobbed around in the green. It was Bonny. She was trotting around and around her fence, looking for a way out.

We circled around and back.

Now Bonny was working on the gate. First, she pushed her nose against it. Then she turned tail and pushed with her rump. The gate began to give.

I asked, "Why does Bonny want out?"

And Pegasus answered in a big, windy voice, "She wants to foal free, on the meadows."

10 I came wide awake. Rain poured down the window pane. Thunder roared like a bulldozer over the town. My heart thumped as if I had been running.

I knew that what Pegasus said was true. Bonny was out in the storm, having her foal.

At first, I was too tense and tight to move. After a while, I loosened up and climbed out of bed. My jeans and shirt were piled on the table. I pulled them on and stole out to the kitchen.

My folks slept with their door open. I couldn't turn on the light. I crept carefully around the table toward the door. In the deep dark, I couldn't see a thing, not an outline or a reflection. I stumbled on Lad.

93

He started up, growling.

"Shhh! It's me!" I let him sniff me. Then he licked my hand. I edged around him and opened the door.

Pounding rain echoed in the kitchen. I dodged outside and shut the door on Lad's tail. He squealed.

Quickly, I pulled him outside with me and drew the door shut again. "All right, come if you want. I've got to hurry."

The steps were slippery, the ground at the bottom was mud. I hadn't bothered with sneakers. Cold mud stung my feet as I ran for Rusty.

I pedaled hard along the street into the driving rain. The street was empty, rain-shiny under the streetlights. All the houses were dark. There was no sound but the rush of rain. Off to my left, the town was a blur of dim lights. On my right, the meadows were dark gray.

"It's morning," I thought. A sort of dawn was creeping up behind the rain.

I pumped into the driveway. There were no

streetlights here. I pedaled through dimness. Behind me, Lad panted and splashed.

The bridge rumbled under my tires. I could barely see the stream, swollen twice its size, swirling under. The ducks must have been asleep.

Up ahead, the Greek temple showed a light.

I was surprised. The Jasons, up before anybody else? Then I forgot about them. "Bonny!" I called into the rain, "I'm coming!"

The gate was down.

Looking about the dark gray paddock, I saw no hump or mound of Bonny. She must be loose in the meadows.

I dropped Rusty. "Lad, stay here. Stay." Lad might upset Bonny. I had a feeling she might be easily upset. I hated to leave him sitting in a puddle, but it was his fault. He didn't have to come.

I ran around the house. The rain was letting up, but mud splashed in my face. "Bonny! Bonny Bun!"

Mist and rain lifted like a curtain. I saw the

95

outlines of the meadows, gray in half-light. I glimpsed a lighter gray smudge, way out. It was tiny among hills and hollows. It was Bonny.

I slogged out toward her.

The closer I came, the slower I slogged. A morning breeze sifted through the light rain. Grass turned green as I stumbled through it. The sky over the meadows was a cloud-mass, gray as Bonny. But over the town, blue sky was opening up.

"Bonny!"

She raised her head. She twitched her ears, so I knew she heard me. But she did not move to come to me.

Fifty yards off, I felt a difference.

It was a different feeling in the air, like a smell.

At thirty yards, I hit the difference.

Waves of quiet washed around me.

I was splashing, shouting, into an ocean of peace. I struggled to keep active. "Bonny!" I yelled, one last time. Then my voice died. I gave up struggling and splashing. The waves of quietness lapped higher. I went forward gently, through an air I had never breathed before.

The ocean of peace was brighter than sunlight. I saw gray all around me, splattering rain. But inside, I was sunshine. I heard the beginnings of traffic out on the street. But inside, I was silence. I had no notion how long I stood and watched Bonny. Time did not tick. The world did not turn on its axis.

Quietly, Bonny watched me. Then she turned away and grazed, nosing the sopping grass. The foal hung out, half-born.

He was flat and darkly shiny. He wiggled and slipped out and dropped in the grass. Bonny grazed.

The foal was packaged in slime. Silently, he flopped about, trying to unfold his legs.

Very slowly, Bonny turned to him. She licked his face, lifting off the slime. Between licks, she grazed around him. Her dainty hoofs looked huge and heavy, stepping carelessly

around the foal. She was in no hurry at all to look after him. How could she hurry? Time had stopped.

She licked the foal's nose, and he breathed. He made a weak, trembly noise and kicked free of his packaging. Long, bony legs like sticks sprawled.

Bonny grazed. Sometimes she looked absently at me. Sometimes she turned back to the foal. More and more she returned to him, more and more she licked him. She breathed over him, muttering. His slime-slicked coat began to fluff. Breathing, he rounded out. Now I wondered how he could ever have fit inside Bonny.

His coat was pale, pale gray, almost white. He had a wisp of white mane, and a rabbity, cotton fluff tail. He looked at the wet world calmly. It didn't seem to surprise him. I wondered if his world was coded in his genes, the same as his shape and color. He seemed almost to know what to expect.

He seemed to know, too, what to do. His legs were going to be his life. He couldn't wait to start using them. He shrugged and kicked.

He pushed with his weak hind legs till he almost stood up. Then he flopped.

Rain still drizzled. But around us a sun seemed to glow. Early trucks rumbled on the street and birds cheeped in the meadow bushes. Around us, silence hummed.

Bonny grazed. The foal managed to stand. He wobbled and swayed. Twice he fell down. But he struggled right back up. He staggered after Bonny, who had moved a few steps away.

He nuzzled her side. He sucked at her shoulder. She swung around quick, and nipped him.

The foal jerked back. He seemed as surprised as I was. He almost fell. But he spread his legs and stayed upright. Bonny stepped away. The foal followed and tried again. He didn't discourage easily! This time he found the teat.

Bonny looked around at him. "Don't bite him," I cried.

She didn't need me to tell her. She looked at the foal now, softly. She licked his trembling cotton tail. And with that, I came down to earth. Time started ticking. I noticed the drizzle, and my mud-shod bare feet. The earth turned on its axis, and I saw it was full morning.

"Bonny," I said, "you shouldn't be out here! You should be safe in your paddock. Why'd you break out?" I moved toward her.

She shied away. The foal staggered. He saw me coming and tried to turn away. Here was another thing he knew, somehow. I was not Horse.

I hesitated. They didn't want me. They were happy, being Horse together. I was an outsider.

If I had been Angel, I think Bonny would have kicked. She was just getting to know her foal. They were beginning to relate. And here this bossy human had to come and butt in! I didn't blame Bonny for lifting her lip at me.

But that was all she did. We were best friends. She let me come up and take hold of her halter. "Come on, Bonny Bun. We're going home."

I led her very slowly toward the Greek temple. The foal came tottering after. He had never walked on grass before. He had never breathed before. But he knew how to walk, to eat, and to follow Bonny. Watching him over my shoulder, I saw him gain strength. By the time we reached the downed gate, he was walking pretty steadily.

He couldn't quite aim himself between the gateposts. I pushed him through with my hands on his sides. I turned Bonny loose inside the paddock. Then I propped up the gate. It wouldn't hold Bonny. But I thought she would stay near the foal.

I heard noises from the temple. A phone rang. Someone ran upstairs. "Good-bye, Bonny," I said softly. "I'll be back later." I went back to Lad and Rusty.

I lifted Rusty out of the puddle. "Come on, Lad, let's get out of here." I was halfway to the saddle when the front door burst open.

11   The door banged open as though it had been kicked. "Hey, you!" Mr. Jason roared. "You with the dog! You, Pat!"

I almost jumped on Rusty and pushed off fast. But if I did that, I couldn't come back and see my Bonny again. I trembled beside Rusty while Mr. Jason stormed out onto the porch.

He yelled, "I want to know where my Angel is!"

"Angel?"

"I bet you know where!"

Lad growled.

"I don't know, Mr. Jason. I thought she was in bed."

"Then what are you here for?" He jumped

down off the porch and strode toward us. Lad growled louder.

"I'm here for Bonny. She——"

"Look, Angel never came home last night." Mr. Jason stopped, with an eye on Lad. His good-looking face was crumpled. He looked old. "You're the only friend she has coming around. I bet you know where she went."

"Honest, I don't know." My knees shook. I gripped the handlebars tight. Lad came between us, hackles up. Lad was scared, and so was I. But I was also kind of sorry for Mr. Jason. Angel hadn't come home all night. I wondered what my dad would do if I didn't come home all night. Looked at like that, Mr. Jason didn't seem so fierce, after all. He just seemed more of a dad than before.

Mrs. Jason stumbled out onto the porch and wrapped herself around a pillar. She wore a slinky pink bathrobe and curlers. Even at that distance, I could see she had been crying.

"Mr. Jason." I swallowed. "Maybe Angel's out with Letty."

"Letty?"

"On the Honda."

"What?"

"I heard a motorcycle last night."

"*What are you talking about?*"

I cleared a lump out of my throat. "Mr. Jason, you know you saw me on a motorbike with a fellow?"

"I remember."

"Well, that wasn't me you saw."

He sure caught on fast! "That was Angel?"

I nodded.

"Angel in your scarf. I see. And it was you riding the pony."

I nodded.

Back on the porch, Mrs. Jason sobbed.

I couldn't stand it. I said, "Angel was talking about running away. But Letty said he couldn't afford it. I bet they'll be back."

On the street, a truck shifted gears and slowed down. We all turned to look. Dad's red pickup swung around the turn and charged up the driveway.

Mr. Jason asked, "That your folks?"

"I guess."

"So you weren't home last night, either."

"Oh yes, I was."

The pickup rumbled over the bridge. Ducks sprang up in pairs, quacking disaster and danger. Up the hill, Dad drove like a drag racer and slammed on the brake. He cut the engine and leaped out. "What the heck are you doing here at this hour?"

"I came for Bonny. She——"

"Your mother is having kittens. I knew you were here, but she thought you'd been kidnapped!"

"I'm awfully sorry. But Bonny——"

Mrs. Jason ran down the steps. Bathrobe flying, eyes streaming, she rushed up to Dad. "Have you seen Angela? Angela never came home at all!"

Dad turned to her. Puzzled, he glanced from her to Mr. Jason to me.

Mr. Jason opened his mouth. Before he could speak, another engine slowed on the street. We swung around.

Letty's Honda roared into the driveway and over the bridge, through a cloud of hysterical

106

ducks. Letty, crouched in front, was completely hidden in armor. All we saw of Angel was a flying mist of blond hair and two small arms clutching Letty's waist.

Mrs. Jason shrieked, "It's *her*! It's *her*!" She ran down the driveway, arms outstretched, pink robe fluttering.

Mr. Jason raised his fists and shook them. He growled much louder than Lad.

Letty surely couldn't hear the shrieks or the growls. He must have seen, first, the fluttering pink, and then the fists.

The Honda leaned and slanted away, off the driveway. It leaped a hillock, bounced, slid on the wet grass. It recovered and jounced off across the meadow. I guessed Letty meant to circle back to the street.

Dad cried, "No! No!" I was startled to see him run, waving, after the Honda.

Mr. Jason pounded after him.

Mrs. Jason stopped running halfway down the driveway. Watching, she gripped her throat in her hands.

The Honda slid and lurched across the wet

meadow. Letty leaned and turned, circling, and then I saw. He was headed for the low hill that hid the new cellar hole.

The Honda hit the hill.

I heard myself yelling, "No, no!"

The Honda soared over the hill and dropped out of sight. It did not show again. But we still heard the engine. It whined like a trapped animal, trying to claw its way free.

12   The hospital was quiet. Quiet footsteps fell softly on the tile. The walls of the long hall where we sat were a quiet, tan shade. There were no windows. Quiet lights glowed in the ceiling. This quiet was nothing like the quiet in the meadow with Bonny. There, time had stopped ticking. Here, time ticked dreadfully, dreadfully slowly.

A white, starched nurse sat at a big desk at one end of the hall. Passing doctors laughed with her at quiet jokes. A woman in blue pushed a trolley of quietly clinking glasses down the hall. A nurse swished by us, quiet as a ghost in thick-soled shoes. She smiled at Marty. From the ceiling, a cold quiet voice said, "Click. Dr. Grayson, 6–B, Dr. Grayson. Dr. Larat, 10–4. Dr. Larat."

Mrs. Jason lifted her tear-stained face. "That's our doctor, Larat. Why are they calling our doctor?"

Mom patted her hand. "Don't worry. He'll finish up on the kids first."

"They're calling Dr. Larat," Mrs. Jason insisted. Mom went on patting her.

"Click," said the ceiling, "Dr. Romanski, 10–4."

"Patty," Mom said, "Take Marty? He's getting restless. Walk him up and down."

No wonder Marty was getting restless. The clock over the desk said two o'clock. We had been there since nine. Mom and Mrs. Jason sat together against the wall. Across from them, Mr. Jason and Dad sat slumped under a NO SMOKING sign. Dad fingered his empty pipe. Mr. Jason stared down at his twisting hands.

I stood up and lifted Marty to my shoulder, so he could see something as we walked. I walked him slowly away from the desk, toward the swinging doors at the other end of the hall. I walked dancingly, accenting every step. That way, Marty thought there was something new and interesting going on.

A sign on the door said NO ADMITTANCE.

Behind the doors, Dr. Larat and a couple of nurses were working on Angel and Letty. Or maybe they had gone out for a coffee break. There was no sound from beyond the swinging doors.

Marty and I swayed outside it. Marty gurgled and wiggled. I swayed like a meadow weed in the wind. "Hush, Marty, please. 'All the pretty little horses.' Shhh."

There was silence behind the doors, but I could see light through the chink. I shifted Marty to my other side. "Please, God," I said inside, "don't let them die!"

Nobody had said much to me. They got the story out of me, and then they were silent. Nobody scolded. Nobody said, "If those two die . . ."

I couldn't stop thinking about it. Over and over, I saw myself putting on Angel's red coat. I saw myself galloping away from Mr. Jason, who thought I was Angel. I saw Angel tying my scarf over her shining hair.

Over and over, I saw the cellar hole. It was

112

a mud pit. In one corner, the Honda growled and jerked, trying to dig through the earth wall. The silent heap in the middle was Letty and Angel.

They were so bloody-muddy, we could hardly tell them apart. Dad took over. He wouldn't let us move them; he said it might hurt them more. He knew how to turn off the Honda. He sent Mrs. Jason running to the phone to call the ambulance. Letty and Angel never moved. We weren't sure they breathed.

When I couldn't stand this a minute longer, I made myself think about Bonny's new foal. I closed my eyes and breathed Marty's warm smell. And inside my head, I saw the little foal balancing on wobbly stick-legs, looking at the world. I told myself, "He's the reason I did it. He wouldn't be here if I hadn't done what Angel wanted." And I hadn't known he would be so wonderful! I hadn't expected any disaster, either. I thought, "Must be I'm dumb. I'm so dumb, it isn't my fault."

The doors swung open.

I stepped back.

EMERGENCY
ROOM

A man in a white coat backed out, pulling a trolley. On the trolley lay a bandage roll under a sheet. Two stiff big casts stuck out, one on each side. Angel's hair spilled over the end of the trolley.

I looked back up the hall. They were getting up. They came slowly, jostling each other, like a flock of worried ducks. They surrounded the trolley.

The doors swung again. Dr. Larat came through. He was a big man. But before the doors swung shut, I glimpsed another trolley behind him. Letty's head poked out from under the sheet. His hair had been chopped short. The scalp was a mass of blood.

My stomach knotted up. I thought I would be sick on the shiny tiles. While I fought it, Dr. Larat murmured to the Jasons. "Concussion . . . femur . . . fracture." Then the big doctor turned round to me.

I expected him to say, "So you're the one responsible, eh?"

He asked me, "Can you tell us about the young man?"

The young man?

Mr. Jason mumbled, "Letty."

Oh, Letty! I couldn't tell them anything. I didn't know his address, whether he worked or went to school, his name. "Very well," Dr. Larat said, "we'll ask him when he's conscious."

He barreled off down the hall, white coat billowing. As he went, the ceiling said, "Click. Dr. Larat, 5–20."

"We'll ask him when he's conscious." Then Letty would be conscious! And by the look of the Jasons, Angel would, too.

They leaned together. They hugged and patted each other. They smiled and cried.

Angel on the trolley and the white coat and Mrs. Jason went away in the elevator. Mr. Jason walked us to the front door.

"You folks have been great," he said, "Just great." He mopped up his tears with a big red handkerchief. "I won't forget this!"

"Neither will we," Mom commented as we bumped home in the pickup. "Neither will we!"

116

13 In a way, they did forget. They forgot to scold. The sermon I waited for never came. Nobody said boo. If they thought I didn't need their scolding, they were darned right. I deserved it, but I sure didn't need it.

Mom went to the hospital now and then with Mrs. Jason. I was glad to babysit. The worse Marty fussed and squalled, the better I liked it. I knew I deserved it.

One day Mom said, "You go this time. You can cut the tulips for Angel."

I was startled. "Your tulips?"

Under the stairs, the tulips were soft and bright. Rosy sunlight streamed through their petals. Mom liked to stand and look at them,

117

after thinning lettuce. I said again, "Your tulips!"

Mom said bravely, "They'll bloom again, next year."

I cut the tulips. They glowed rich and fuzzy. Their petals felt like Marty's skin. I cut them, piled them in Rusty's basket, and pedaled downtown to the hospital.

"You came on your bicycle?" Mrs. Jason sounded very surprised. She sat by Angel's bed, twirling her necklace. She sat straight and seemed cold sober.

I had never been in a hospital room before. While I tried to be polite, I looked around sharp. The walls were pale, like downstairs. The floors were tiled. An old woman slept in the other bed in Angel's room. I wondered what they talked about, alone together. Footsteps and voices passed in the hall. Dishes clinked on trolleys. The ceiling clicked and called for Dr. Pomeroy, Dr. Larat, and Dr. Jones.

I said, "You aren't lonesome!"

Angel smiled.

She was in traction. One foot was suspended from the ceiling. She had a heavy cast on it and on one arm. Her head was still bandaged. She looked flat, miserable, and very bored.

I said, "I brought you something." I produced the tulips.

Angel sighed.

Mrs. Jason popped up. "How lovely! Home-grown, aren't they? I'll get them a vase. . . ." She rushed off, leaving me alone, looking sadly down at Angel.

Angel said, "I bet you're taking care of Bonny."

"Of course!"

"Did she ever have the foal?" she asked politely.

"Haven't you heard? She had it the day you . . ."

"Cracked up. Mmmm."

I told her, "He's a colt. He's pale gray, got a tail like a rabbit. You should see him hop around!"

"Mmmm."

"He's got this baby fur, soft like velveteen."

119

"Are you going to see Letty?"

"I don't know." I didn't plan to. "Where is he?"

"Mom knows. She goes to see him."

"She does?"

"He doesn't have any family."

"How is he?" I tried not to remember him, all blood.

"Fractures. I bet he'll be out of here before I am!"

"When'll you be out?"

"Doctor won't say."

Mrs. Jason brought back the tulips in a vase. "Look, Angela, I'll put them here so you can look at them."

Angel smiled. "Nothing like looking at flowers all day!"

Mrs. Jason turned to me. "Patricia, I want to thank you for looking after Angel's pony."

Angel laughed. Then she made a face. Laughing hurt. "You don't have to thank Pat for that. Everything Pat ever did with me, she did it for the pony."

Mrs. Jason asked me seriously, "Is that true,

120

Patricia? Do you like the pony?"

"Oh, I love Bonny!"

Mrs. Jason narrowed her eyes at me. She looked like Angel, getting an idea. "Well," she said at last, "we can't keep the pony. Angela won't be riding for a while. I'll talk to Mr. Jason about it."

Did she mean what I hoped she meant?

The ceiling clicked and said, "Visiting hours are over." It was a great relief.

The next day Mr. Jason said, "You can have the ponies." He said, "You can have them for free. Just take them off my hands."

I looked over at Bonny, grazing in the paddock. The foal was curled up asleep in her shadow. Noon sun shimmered on her gray, satin coat. Her slim side was white-dappled, like water in sun. She swished her tail and looked back at me. She nickered hello.

"Bonny," I called, "you're going to stay with me! You'll be with me forever! Good-bye, now. I'll be back!" I leaped on Rusty and pumped all the way home.

My folks sat together on the outside stairs,

drinking coffee. Dad had just knocked off
work. Mom had been gardening. She cradled
her cup in earth-stained hands and watched
the garden lovingly. I would watch Bonny like
that.

I leaned Rusty against the stairs and sat
down by Mom. I tried to sound calm, but my
voice squeaked. "Mr. Jason says I can have the
ponies!"

"Oh yes?" Dad's cold tone should have
warned me.

"I'll get a paper route," I promised. "They
won't cost you a cent! All we have to do is take
out the cellar stairs and put up a fence."

Mom tore her gaze from the garden. She
looked around at me.

Dad set down his cup and brought out his
pipe.

I said, softer, "Couldn't we?"

Dad said, "You've got to be crazy."

I saw then that I had been crazy, ever since
Mr. Jason said, "You can have the ponies." It
wasn't only the money, or the fact that we
would be moving. It was everything that had

happened. All right, I deserved it. But what about Bonny?

I said, "Mr. Jason says if we don't take them, he's going to put an ad in the paper."

Dad lit his pipe. "Good idea."

"But suppose the people who . . . buy them . . . don't . . . love them."

Mom set down her cup. She laid an earthy hand on my knee, not gently, hard. I blinked back the tears that were swimming around.

She said, "People buy ponies because they want them."

"Angel didn't want Bonny!"

"That doesn't often happen. Whoever buys these ponies will want them. And pretty soon, he'll love them. You aren't the only one in the world who can love!" When Mom saw I wouldn't cry, she lifted her hand a bit, patting my knee. "You did a great thing for Bonny. You made sure the foal was born safe and well. Now he's here in the world with us, he'll live his own life. He'll have to take his chances, like us. See?"

I nodded.

I still went over to the Jasons to chore every day. I fed Bonny and watered her. I brushed her till she shone like ripply water. Her mane and tail fluffed out like dandelion puffs. I made a rope halter for the foal. The Book said he should wear a halter very young, so he would grow up tame. It was one thing to tie the halter on his little head. It was another thing to lead him. We had some tugs of war in that paddock! Bonny watched us kindly. She seemed to laugh at us.

The foal grew strong, fast. At first he stayed always close to Bonny. He trotted at her heels and napped under her as she grazed. When he was ten days and three hours old, he tried to eat grass. His little muzzle pushed among the grasses, alongside Bonny's. But he didn't know yet what it was about. He looked up at me. His eyes were soft under long, curly lashes. A wet grass blade lay across his nose. But there was no grass in his mouth.

I went there for the last time, the day Mr.

Jason told me he had sold the ponies. The man was coming that night to take them away.

That day, the foal left Bonny's side.

I leaned on the fence, watching Bonny graze. The foal bounded in circles around her. He bounced stiffly, as though he had wire springs in his legs. He held his legs straight and his neck arched. His fluff-tail floated out behind. Wider and wider he circled, farther and farther away from Bonny.

He had never been so far from her before. He broke away and started a whole new circle, not around Bonny. This circle, too, widened farther and farther. The foal soared stronger, higher. He seemed to float. In a minute he would fly, like Pegasus.

Now Bonny looked up. She noticed how far the foal had gone. She nickered to him. He floated on around his wide, airy circle.

Bonny ambled over to him. In the middle of a bound, he stopped. He nuzzled up against her. Then he sucked, flicking his silly tail. He was so tired, his bony hocks knocked together.

I leaned on the fence and watched my

126

ponies. They would always be mine. They were a part of me, I was a part of them. We belonged to each other for always.

I went about the chores.

When I left, I called Bonny. She came trotting to the fence. I took her lovely Arabian head in my hands and kissed her velvet nose. She looked at me softly. The foal came and reared against the fence. I patted the baby fur on his forehead. He jumped away. He didn't like to be touched. Bonny blew gently and rested her head on my shoulder.

After a long, bright time I moved away. I said, "Good-bye, Bonny." Then I added the words she expected to hear from me. "I'll be back."

Though I knew I would never be back.